To Larry with all good wishes — Constance Levy 1997

WITHDRAWN

WHEN
WHALES
EXHALE

AND
OTHER POEMS

Also by Constance Levy

*I'm Going to Pet a Worm Today
and Other Poems*
illustrated by Ronald Himler

A Tree Place and Other Poems
illustrated by Robert Sabuda

WHEN WHALES EXHALE

AND OTHER POEMS

CONSTANCE LEVY

ILLUSTRATIONS BY JUDY LaBRASCA

Margaret K. McElderry Books

To Freda Fireside, Aaron, Adam, Benjamin,
and always, Monty
—C. L.

Margaret K. McElderry Books
An imprint of Simon & Schuster Children's Publishing Division
1230 Avenue of the Americas
New York, New York 10020

Text copyright © 1996 by Constance Kling Levy
Illustrations copyright © 1996 by Judy LaBrasca

Book design by Becky Terhune
The text of this book is set in Futura
The illustrations were rendered in gouache

Printed and bound in the United States of America

First Edition

10 9 8 7 6 5 4 3 2 1

Library of Congress Cataloging-in-Publication Data

Levy, Constance.
When whales exhale and other poems / Constance Levy ; illustrated by Judy
LaBrasca.—1st ed.
p.   cm.
Summary: A collection of poems about the natural world, including "Looking at
Mushrooms," "Bear Feet," and "Eating Potato Chips on a Mountain."
ISBN 0-689-80946-8
1. Nature—Juvenile poetry. 2. Children's poetry, American. [1. Nature—Poetry.
2. American poetry.] I. Title.
PS3562.E9256W48   1996
811'.54—dc20
95-52560
CIP
AC

Contents

Sea Swimmer

The water salts my lips.
It's quiet here,
and I am wrapped in cool
and silky blue.

Below me,
flicking silver-sparkled tails,
a school of tiny fish
comes racing through.

I see my hand
reach down to them;
it stops
and lingers

to feel their touch,
like kisses,
as they slip
between
my fingers.

A Camel Ride in the Desert

Climb aboard
while it is resting;
when it lifts you
you will slide.
Hold the hump tight.
Wear your hat,
or soon you'll think
your head is fried.
You may whisper,
you may hum,
you may mutter,
you may sing,
but the camel will ignore you
and not utter anything.

There is silence in the desert
and a sameness to the land:
lots of sun
and miles and miles
of peanut butter–colored sand.

Wild Blueberries

All I think of
now is berries,
blue and ripe
and ready berries,
as I'm climbing up
the hillside
picking berries,
and I eat,

first politely,
then by handfuls.
Bring a bucket
and we'll meet

on the hilltop.
We're in luck, it's
very berry
summer sweet!

Lunch Hour

This morning
a cloud
and a three minute
shower;
now, sunlight
at noon
and the lunch hour
crowd:
ladybug, butterfly,
horsefly and bee,
all taking quick sips
from the same
pink flower.

Looking at Mushrooms

Some say the mushrooms
dropped
from outer space.
Some say they're weird.
My friend says
once one spoke to him.

I think they're funny;
look at them
      guarding the rotting leaves,
      camping on trees,
      snapping themselves on logs
      like frogs.
Such creatures of whim!

And that one
with the floppy hat,
did you see him peek,
just then,
from under the brim?

Hawk in the Tree

One look at Hawk's
stern face,
the fierce hooked beak,
the motionless shape
in the crook of a tree,
keen and sharp and sure,

and I am
shoulder to shoulder
with the mouse,

I feel the squirrel's
fear,

even the snake's
cold blood
turning colder.

Under the Crab Apple Tree

A crab apple fell,
bounced on my head,
and dropped to the mud
with a muffled thud.

Gave me a start,
but I'm O.K.
Nothing bruised and
nothing broke.

Just a
slapstick
crab apple joke.

Finding a Piece of Robin's Egg

It could be a piece
of a porcelain cup,
this shard of sky-blue shell,
smooth and delicate and thin.
I lift it gently
and it cracks;
with every touch
it cracks again.
It weighs a feather,
if that much.

So frail a thing,
it makes you think
how awfully hard
it must have tried
to summon up the strength
to hold
a growing baby bird inside.

Passengers

The ship is a stranger
on the sea
no matter how many times
it sails,
and the passengers
who walk the decks
and hold on tightly
to the rails
look out at water,
vast and wild,
and rock with the waves
that rise and fall
and feel very, very,
very
small.

When Whales Exhale
(Whale Watching)

There's a horn sound
from the blowhole
and a high-speed spout
when a whale at sea
blasts the old air out.
It breathes up a geyser,
a flare of fizz,
a white cloud that shows you
where it is
in the endless waves
of the great green sea.
Oh, whales exhale
magnificently!

Tail Flukes

The humpback whale will charm you
with the ballet of its dive,
shaping itself
like the downstroke
of a wave,
its tail flukes,
great butterfly wings,
spread wide.

Glacier

Miles wide
and fathoms deep,
ice skin,
ice bones,
the glacier creeps
slowly over the land
it thinks it owns,

carves valleys,
bites mountains,
chews rocks,
sweeps pieces
with it
as it goes,

weeps
from too much sun,
and drops
big boulders
miles from home.

It never stops,
though you could watch it
for a year
and think it
sleeps . . .

Water Rings

What a beautiful sight!
The sun beaming,
the sky teeming with wings,
the earth holding
this glassy pond
like a plate
in its green palm.

I will take
what it offers me:
a feast of water rings
    that frog dips
    and bug sips
    and fishes' kisses
    make.

Eclipse

The sky grew
strangely dim
when the moon
on its slow walk
stood
smack in front
of the sun
like a dark mask

leaving only
a slim rim
of sun-skin
showing,

a ring
of glowing
gold.

On a Little Island

It's such a little island,
just a button on the sea,
a rocky place where grasses grow
wild and tall and free,
and seagulls take their seafood lunch
to dine here peacefully.

A vacant small white cottage
stands inland from the shore
where once somebody harvested
potatoes, beans, and more.

I wonder why they came here.
I wonder why they've gone,
and if they ever think about
the house they left alone

or miss the wind that whistles by,
the waves that splash and roar,
and the hollyhocks still visiting
beside the faded door.

The Pearl

The truth of this pearl
is that an oyster
cleaning house
wrapped up a bit of grit,

gave it the luster
of the moon
and the texture of a tooth
and made a jewel,

a lively one
that rolls around my palm
when I am barely
moving it.

W o r m   O u t

Poor weary worms
after the rain
squirmed out
and can't squirm back again.

I don't know why,
but I wish they'd try.
(They look so dry!)

The sidewalk is hard,
the sun so bright;
why did they leave
their soft
dark
home

to roam
last night?

Looks bad for them,
too late for some,
but I'll try
to save
this
w
 i
   g
 l g
   y
one . . .

Bear Feet

Suppose
you're in a forest place,
with ferns
and pines
and berries,
and find that you
are face to face
with two fresh
bear prints
pressed in mud,
at least the size
of a baseball glove.

Suppose your eyes
trace each round toe,
and you just know
the bear is BIG,
a bear that heard you come
and hid,
and left its bear smell
in the air.

Well, would your stomach
turn to lumps,
and would your heart go
wild with thumps?
Mine would, and once
it *did*, it *did!*

What to Do on a Mountain Top

Take yourself
to a mountain top
windcooled and sunwarmed
and very high;
watch seagulls
and think
how it feels to fly.
Look over the land
with a mountain's eye.

Set your thoughts free
to drift, to roam.
Be comfortable;
feel right at home,
and help yourself
to some
really fresh
sky . . .

Eating Potato Chips
on a Mountain

The climb was hard but fun,
the rocky trail leading us
with snake twists
and steep rises,
surprises at every turn,
boulders
and fallen trees
and narrow ridges
and cool morning mist
chased off by the sun.

I'm resting on a boulder
eating chips,
licking the oil and salt from my lips.
An ant on my shirt
is nibbling a crumb.

Raining

It rained an ocean yesterday.
It poured the day before,
and now it's raining more!

I'll get a splitting
rainache
if it doesn't turn off soon.
I'm so sun-hungry
I could eat
a whole bright
afternoon!

Autumn Lets Loose

Out of the trees
with every gust
leaves are swirling
as wild as dust,

while closer to earth
petals fall
and seedpods burst.

There's a letting go,
a loosening;
everything longs
to be free, to fly . . .
and suddenly, suddenly,
so do I!